James Talboys Wheeler

The Alchymist's Heir

A Romance in Three Cantos

James Talboys Wheeler

The Alchymist's Heir
A Romance in Three Cantos

ISBN/EAN: 9783337348656

Printed in Europe, USA, Canada, Australia, Japan

Cover: Foto ©Andreas Hilbeck / pixelio.de

More available books at **www.hansebooks.com**

THE
ALCHYMIST'S HEIR.

A

Romance in three Cantos.

--- ---

BY

J. TALBOYS WHEELER.

"I wed with thee! I bound by pr at act
Your bride, so r bond wel n t th af th   ld
That r   the world were pack'l to make yo r r wu,
And every   oken tong e sho ld lord yo.. S r,
Your faschoo l and y r face are loaths   t us:
We tramp! on y   r ffer and on you:
Reg us : we w .. ot l ok poa yo more."

Ta MT

MADRAS:

PRINTED BY PHAROAH AND CO

ATHENÆUM PRESS, MOUNT ROAD.

1802.

PREFACE.

—

The following poem was written fourteen years ago, and is now printed and published for the first time. It would be mere waste of words to assign any reason for the present publication, so distant from the time and place where the tale was originally written. It will be sufficient to say that about two years ago a lamented artist commenced the preparation of a series of *etchings* to illustrate the story, but died before his task was half completed. Accordingly one of these *etchings* has been selected to serve both as a frontispiece to the present edition, and as a memorial of a departed friend. Without therefore any formal dedication, it will be sufficient to say that the author desires to connect his present poem with the name of

ARCHIBALD COLE.

MADRAS,
25th December 1861.

THE ALCHYMIST'S HEIR.

Canto I.

I.

No cunning monk shall hear my tale,
   No coward priest shall see my tears ;
My heart may burst, my life blood fail,
   Before I own their creed or fears.
But on this page each woe I'll trace,
And spirits of the past I'll face,
Till memory's sting hath lost its power,
   And thought hath ceased to burn my breast ;
I fain would live one calmer hour
   Ere in the grave I seek my rest.

II.

There was a time, but oh how brief !
Ere yet I recked of crime or grief ;
When free as air I roved the hills
With conscience clear as mountain rills :
It passed !—I longed for glory, fame,
A warrior's crown and soldier's name ;
Then love transformed each high design
And chained my soul at beauty's shrine ;
I loved, and lived upon the light
Of passion's dream and fancies bright,
And moved as in a heavenly land
Lit with a beam from angel hand.

III.

I was a college student then,
And read the gathered lore of men,
O'er ancient bards and sages hung,
And learnt me many a bygone tongue ;
For she, the idol of my dreams,
Would set at nought my boyish themes,
Would scorn the love sick strain, and sneer
At martial tales of strife and fear ;
But oft would list with flashing eyes
To olden lays and histories,
Of times when tyrants crouched at bay
 Before the might of deathless mind,
And priest and despot felt the sway
 Of reason which they could not bind ;
When patriot's voice and poet's song
Could shield the good and banish wrong.
And dauntless genius, pure and free,
Ne'er bent the knee to tyranny ;
Whilst freedom soared on wings of thought
By chains unbound, by gold unbought.

Such tales she loved to hear me tell
 And such she fondly hoped for me ;
Till my own madness broke the spell
 And changed each joy to misery.

IV.

One night, whilst in my lonely room,
 I heard a horse's tramp beneath :
They brought me news of sudden doom,
 My nearest kin was near to death.
He was the brother of my sire,
An ancient man with glance of fire,

Who lived apart from worldly din
And never saw his kind or kin,
But practised arts most dire to see
In magic and in alchymy.
Yet when I was an orphan left,
Of parents, wealth, and all bereft,
That man became, though strange and wild,
A father to his brother's child.
So at that midnight time I sped
To seek that old man's dying bed,
Hear the last words and close the eyes
Of him who dealt in mysteries,
Who still was wise, and once was great,
Yet could not steal one day from fate.

v.

Heavens, what a storm of fearful power
Revelled abroad at that dark hour !
The thunder roared and lightning flashed,
   As though the spirits of the night
In angry warfare howled and clashed,
   And battled with unearthly might ;
Whilst viewless armies onward came
On rolling cars and steeds of flame,
Till mountain, forest, hill, and sky
Were shook by heaven's artillery.
Amid this grim and awful gloom
   I reached a tower all lone and bare ;
And entered Alcar's dreary room
   Trembling with fear and grief and care.
A shrunken form lay on the bed
With clammy cheek and lips of dread ;
Drawing with frightful toil each breath,
And struggling in the grasp of death

With gnashing teeth and clutching fingers,
Whilst yet the life within him lingers ;
Till withered brow and bloodshot eye,
 And bursting veins with madness rife,
Were lit with that fierce energy
 Which burns not save in deathly strife.
No leech or hungry nurse was there,
No priest to shrive by sign or prayer,
No friend nor kin to bend the knee
And soothe his dying agony.
The tempest raged, and livid beams
Of lightning played in fitful gleams,
And thunder shook the tower and hill ;
But in that chamber all was still,
Save the wild fits that tore his frame
As laboured breathings went and came.
I stood beside the fainting man
And wiped the cold sweat as it ran
Adown his brow and shrivelled cheek,
And bent to hear if he could speak ;
But not a sound his lips could utter
Save stifled groan or broken mutter,
A hoarse, convulsive cry, a gasp
Whilst grappled in corruption's grasp ;
Then in his throat I heard the rattle,—
Exulting death had won the battle.

VI.

We live to die we know not when,
 We die to go we know not where,
And God shall judge all mortal men
 And every word and deed declare ;
Yet, on the graves of ages past
 Reckless of all we onward tread ;

No thought upon the future cast,
  No lesson learn from vanished dead.
And life is but a wearying breath,
A battling with our fate and death,
A toiling thro' an unknown clime
Twixt two eternities of time ;
With heart and soul in constant jar,
  With spirit panting to be free,
Oppressed by doubts of what we are
  And fears of what we soon must be.
And 'tis this very dread which breeds
Our endless dreams and countless creeds,
And thwarts the best and bravest minds
  Whom tyrant rule could ne'er appal,
Who fain would burst the chain which binds
  Man's conscience in a human thrall.

VII.

Awe-struck I gazed upon the dead,
  When lo ! amid the fearful gloom,
A withered crone approached the bed,
  To dress that body for the tomb.
I sickened at the ghastly sight,
And turned to gaze upon the night ;
Yet still by some mysterious power
I saw the labours of that hour.
Upon the corpse were antique rings
All graven o'er with mystic things,
And closely bound upon his breast
A small clasped volume lay at rest.
The graven relics all I took,
The ancient rings and wondrous book ;
Then rose, and with a softened heart,
I left that room to weep apart
For him I never more should see,
Who aye had been a friend to me.

VIII.

Oh what a balm there is in tears,
   And would that I could shed them now,
And cleanse the stain of guilty years
   Out from my heart and off my brow.
My spirit like to summer flowers
   Is thirsting for this holy dew,
Which cheers the soul in darkest hours
   And gently leads it heavenward too ;
Till every tear drop seems a spell
   To call bright angels from above,
To soothe the breast which sorrows swell,
   To give it peace and teach it love ;
To banish every harsh regret
For sunny hopes in darkness set,
And bring from Eden sweeter flowers
To bloom around life's ruined bowers.
Then, whilst to God and heaven resigned,
Devotion leads the chastened mind
   To that far home beyond the spheres ;
Where friends shall meet with joy for ever,
And shame and sorrow pain them never,
   For God shall wipe away all tears.
Oh could I weep one moment now,
   I too could feel my sins forgiven ;
To woe and penance humbly bow,
   And trust in God and hope in heaven.

IX.

For one whole day I sat and wept
   Within that ancient tower alone ;
And never ate and rarely slept,
   For with me in those walls were none
Save the dead man and dying crone.

It was a dark and dreary place
Built by some chief of bygone race,
Half hidden on a woody hill
   Far, far away from track of men ;
Beside it dashed a mountain rill
   Which fell into a marshy glen.
At evening hour I upward went
And stood upon the battlement,
And gazed upon the ether deep,
And looked adown the forest steep,
And wandered thro' each chamber there,
All dank and ruined, cold and bare.
Then down a stair, far underground
An excavated room I found,
Vaulted and deathly as a tomb,
With one pale lamp to light the gloom.
It was my uncle's secret cell
Where he had practised many a spell ;
Where direful tools in sorcery,
In magic and in chymistry,
Phials, crucibles, and crystal stones,
And labelled jars and skeletons,
Elixirs, oils, and curious clay,
And talismans of powerful ray,
Were ranged about on many a shelf
With hidden stores of chymic pelf.
And then I thought upon the book
Which from that old man's breast I took ;
And down I sat to rest and read
Of glamour lore and magic deed.

x.

It was a dark and dangerous tome
   All written by some hoary sage ;
Whilst many a form of sprite and gnome
   Was pictured on each yellow page,

With antique names and magian lines,
And mighty cabalistic signs.
And on the back all worn and old,
Stamped deep in characters of gold,
These stern portentous words were given,—
" 𝖂𝖍𝖔 𝖗𝖊𝖆𝖉𝖘 𝖙𝖍𝖎𝖘 𝖇𝖔𝖔𝖐 𝖎𝖘 𝖑𝖔𝖘𝖙 𝖙𝖔 𝖍𝖊𝖆𝖛𝖊𝖓 !"

XI.

Scornful and prying straight I read
Whilst hours of evening swiftly sped ;
For 'twas a book of gloomy power
Well suited to that solemn hour.
In every crowded page I saw
Dread things that filled my soul with awe ;
Spells that would raise the viewless forms
Who guide the fury of the storms ;
Charms that would call those shapes to birth
Who dwell beneath the pregnant earth ;
When lo ! upon a fearful leaf
An incantation wild and brief
Fell on my eye like words of flame,
And filled my soul and fired my frame ;
It was a spell with lines and signs
To call those spirits from the mines,
Who mingle earth with sunny beams,
Till gold in sparkling radiance gleams,
By many a stream and mountain way
From Ophir's isle to bright Cathay ;
It was a charm to force each gnome
To bear the treasures of his home,
And bring the wealth of golden lands
Within the reach of mortal hands.
My brain whirled round, my fingers shook
Whilst bending o'er that mighty book :

The means and tools were all around,
The very cell was magic ground ;
Visions of endless glory, power,
Dazzled me at that awful hour ;
And dire to see and dread to tell
I made the charm and read the spell,
And on the floor with mystic lines
I drew the cabalistic signs.

XII.

A midnight horror seized my soul,
   When in that vaulted cave I saw
Huge clouds of smoke around me roll,
   Till every nerve was thrilled with awe.
Yet still I thirsted for the gold,
And onwards read with purpose bold ;
When piercing shriek and dismal yell
Came echoing through that lonely cell ;
And lo ! a train of skeletons
   Of livid light and withered hue,
With sparkling gold upon their bones,
   Burst full upon my feverish view ;
Red crowns were on their skulls, and brands
All glared within their grisly hands ;
Whilst from each hollow eyelet hole,
Where erst had beamed a living soul,
Wild flashes of blue lightning came,
   And threw a light all pale and dread ;
As though some weird electric flame
   Had given life to ancient dead.

XIII.

Oh what a motley troop was there !
Yet in their ghastly shape and stare,

Methought I saw a warning look
And mournfull gaze upon the book ;
But I was sworn in heart to see
The end of all this mystery ;
And though I knew, e'en at that hour,
'Twas tampering with an evil power,
Yet on I read that potent spell,
Reckless alike of heaven or hell.

XIV.

With noiseless step and lingering moans
Vanished those trembling skeletons,
But as each glittering mockery fled,
The invocation still I read ;
When burst forth grating peals of laughter,
With cries and shoutings echoing after ;
And lo ! a strange and dwarfish crew
Danced round in every shape and hue,
With fiery eye and fierce grimace
And ceaseless change on every face.
Around the signs, and round about,
All black as midnight danced the rout ;
When loud these fitful numbers rung
In chorussed sounds from every tongue.

Song of the Spirits of Gold.

I.

Hurrah for bright red gold !
  The god of earth and brine !
For beauty rare and manhood bold
  All worship at his shrine.

He buys all mortal toil ;
  He rules with despot might ;
He takes the fruits and claims the soil,
  And who denies his right ?

II.

He chills the patriot's zeal !
  He conquers freemen bold !
And men who bared their breasts to steel
  Have bowed their necks to gold !
He lights the tyrants' brow !
  He beams in beauty's bower !
And loudest praise and warmest vow
  Are claimed for crown and dower !

III.

But hath red wine more light
  When quaffed from cups of gold?
Are hearts more true or forms more bright
  When decked in glittering mould ?
Doth joy beneath his beam
  Shine brightest, purest, best ?
Or virtue bloom beneath his gleam,
  Or wisdom in his crest ?

XV.

'Twas not the air, nor yet the words,
  That smote the heart with nameless fear ;
  But ' twas the wild and demon sneer
That ran thro' all the changing chords.

As though like devils they were versed
   In all the earthly blots and stains,
With which man's human state is cursed,—
   And all to taunt him with his pains.
But I was mighty at that hour,
And revelled in unearthly power,
And read the spell with angrier tone,
And spoke like monarch on a throne.
I ne'er would list with coward ear
To haughty words or bitter sneer,
Whether they came from fiend or man,
Or Prince's frown, or Angel's ban,
Ay, though the foe I thus would brave
Could doom me to an instant grave.
Hence I arose with book in hand
And dared to face that scoffing band ;
But on the dreary floor I saw,
   Within the circling, screeching crew,
A sight of agonising awe—
   A ghastly corpse of livid hue,
In charnel raiment all arrayed
But never in a charnel laid.
There was a glistening life and light
Gleaming within its eye balls bright,
Though death's corrupting hand had been
Tainting that shrivelled carcase lean.
God ! 'twas my uncle's face and form !
And never since, in feast or storm,
Hath e'er that vision ceased to be
A thing of endless misery ;
But ever from that fearful hour
Hath met my view in hall and bower,
Glared in my dreams from eve till light,
Oppressed my soul from morn till night,
Till like corruptions self it came
Aye burning with a withering flame ;

And pain and anguish filled me ever,
And woe and madness left me never ;
For whilst I thirsted for the morrow,
It only brought fresh stings and sorrow.

XVI.

I saw ! I shrieked !—I cannot tell
One sentence more, but down I fell
On the cold floor insensible.
What moments passed I cannot say,
   But when I woke 'twas dead of night ;
Yet by the lamp I saw there lay
   A heap of gold and treasure bright !
Ay, 'twas a pile of purest gold !
A mass that monarchs might beheld !
Fit for the throne of Eastern king
   When nations tremble at his ned ;
Fit for a shrine where priests might bring
   The image of their idolgod !
Amid the awe and fevering thrill
I stood—a puny mortal still,
And tried to move the shining ore ;
But loads that never mortal bore
Defied my strength and laughed to scorn
The might of man of woman born.
And then, so changed was every thought,
   I scarce could leave that golden cave,
Tho' all from floor to roof was fraught
   With direst secrets of the grave.

XVII.

Upward amid that midnight gloom
Once more I sought the dead man's room,

But no corpse lay upon the bed,
   The body of the sage was gone ;
But lo ! there lay all cold and dead
   The form of that old withered crone.
Away I dashed, I scarce recked where,
Once more adown the broken stair ;
Into the tower I fetched some mould
And heaped it o'er the pile of gold,
To hide it from the passer by
Who might perchance the treasure spy ;
But first I seized as much as e'er
Man's arm could lift or back could bear ;
Then turned to seek some spot where men
Could meet their fellow's glance again.

XVIII.

'Twas still the darkest hour of night,
   I reached a village poor and small ;
And saw no light save pale stars bright,
   And only heard my footstep's fall.
When suddenly arose a sound
Of distant mirth and jovial round,
Which led me to a hostelry
Where troops had met for revelry.
They were a merry generous band,
And greeted me with open hand,
So down I laid my load to rest
And drank to quench my burning breast ;
Then bargained with the Captain there
For a strong, fleet, and matchless mare.
We viewed her by a torch's light—
   A creature of the purest blood
With giant might and black as night—
   I saw and bought her as she stood,

Purchased her like a student bold
And paid the cost in new got gold.

XIX.

She straight was saddled at that hour,
  And on her back my gold I flung,
  Then to the seat I lightly sprung
And spurred her on with cruel power—
On, onwards fleeter than the wind
And feast and feasters left behind.
For sprites and skulls danced to my eyes
With ghostly forms and sorceries ;
And demon eye and ghastly stare
  Gleamed on the stream, or peered through wood,
As though my conscience laboured there
  Beneath some deed of crime of blood.

XX.

With wilder gallop on I rode,
Each vision acting like a goad,
Up the hill side, then down a glen,
Or by some blackened copse again ;
Or up a bank my mare I spurred
And nothing but her trampings heard,
And sped along through greenwood bowers
  All darkened beneath midnight's sway,
Where oft in bright and summer hours
  I'd slept full many a dream away.
But still a chaos filled my soul,
Fiends held me in their dread control ;
A strange unnatural strength possessed
My trembling limbs and boiling breast ;
I burned for wild exciting strife,
Reckless alike of limbs or life ;

As though some outward fire would draw
   The flame from out my tortured mind,
But changed by some mysterious law
   It fanned it like a burning wind.

XXI.

Thus felt I in that lonely night,
   When the deep stillness of the hour,
And solemn stars immortal light,
   Had filled me with a wondrous power :
Parting me   from this lower earth,
Making me feel of demon birth,
Till all my woe and misery
Had linked me to infinity,
And human hopes and joys and fears
Became the things of bygone years.
But lo ! upon the hills a ray
Tinted the eastern skies with gray,
And night with all its cares and dreams
Vanished before the morning beams.
Then from a glen the matin bell
Poured in my ears its holy spell,
And gentler feelings strove to impart
A freshness to my wearied heart,
Which like a harp began to move,
Thrilled with the touch of heavenly love.
Oh whither could my spirit go
To find some balm and peace below,
But then to try if mortal power
Could soothe me in that troubled hour,
See if my soul could feel the smile
Of her who could my heart beguile ?
So in a brook I left each trace
Of awe and anguish from my face,

And softlier sped and gentlier rode
To seek my Hilda's pure abode,—
The shrine where all my joys were kept,
The tomb where all those joys have slept.

———

Canto II.

.

———

I.

THE sun hath risen o'er hill and stream
　And bravely on the woodland shines ;
Pouring alike his new-born beam
　O'er flowery vales and mountain pines ;
Till every ray his glance hath flung
Seems like the words of angel tongue,
All nature's boundless regions thrilling,
All earth's uncounted bosoms filling,
With love and rapture, joy and praise,
And music's best and purest lays.
Ye silent and mysterious voices,
　Whose home so far transcendeth ours,
That like a speck our world rejoices
　Beneath the glory of thy bowers !
No living thing in earthly isles
But greets thee with a thousand smiles !
The glittering moth on wings of light
Shines gaily in his golden flight ;
The merry fish with lightning beams
Darts brightly through his native streams ;
And far in forest haunt and glade,
　The joyous bird from tree to tree
Pours out above the woodland shade
　His morning song of melody ;
Whilst flowers and fruits with radiant eyes
List to the wisdom of the skies.
Nor these alone, but since that morn
　When first creation hung the stars ;
Thy genial rays have aye been borne
　Far onward to their silver cars,

And sphere on sphere hath felt thy glance
On to the bounds of heaven's expanse ;
Teaching the countless orbs to sing
  In one vast chorus to thy light ;
Rousing old nature's self to bring
  New proofs of His eternal might,
Who formed the stars and framed the flowers,
Walled the broad seas and built the bowers.

II.

'Twas on a morn as bright as this
That last I dreamed of earthly bliss,
For pain and guilt have steeled my brow
And nature cannot glad me now ;
But then pure thoughts of peaceful hue
Fell on my heart like morning dew,
And visions of fair Hilda stole
In glowing freshness to my soul.
Onward I rode at that sweet hour
To meet her in the lonely bower,
Where morn and eve on bended knee
She worshipped the Divinity.
Quick to a tree my mare I tied,
And left my treasure at her side ;
For there I caught beneath the shade
  A glimpse of Hilda's radiant charms ;
And swift as thought the blushing maid
  Was caught within her Franco's arms.

III.

Oh ! she was lovely as the stars
When throned upon their silver cars ;

Or when they gaze on man below
   From their bright home of holy shrines,
And seem to weep for human woe
   Whilst constant beauty round them shines.
For Hilda's glances fell like beams
From their bright home of holy dreams,
Where goodness dwelt in saintly eyes
As heaven looks down through starry skies ;
And her chaste soul and lofty mind
In angel loveliness were shrined :
Yet she could weep the purest tears
For all who dwell on earthly spheres,
And he who gazed upon her eyes
Might deem himself in Paradise.
Oh ne'er on earth hath beamed a form
   More fair or spiritually bright,
   Or fancy in its happiest flight
Dreamed of a heart more clear and warm ;
And none hath met a lover's view
More holy, beautiful, or true.

IV.

With kindly glance and blushing sigh
   And voice that made my life-blood thrill,
   " Franco !" she said,—" say, art thou ill ?
" For red and restless is thine eye,
" And pale and throbbing is thy brow,
" And trembling are thy fingers now !"
My uncle's fearful death I told,
His learned skill and stores of gold ;
But not a word of sprite or spell,
Or horrors of his secret cell.
I told her that his dust was laid
Within a convent's sacred shade ;

And I had left his gloomy tower
To seek her in her blooming bower.
I told her that my heart was sad,
  And I was weary of my life ;
And that my soul would ne'er be glad
  But far away from noise and strife ;
And then with all a lover's pride
  I whispered in her gentle ear,
That I was rich and free beside,
And were she now the student's bride,
  We might away with care and fear,
And live apart from wordly kin
And never meet with wordly sin.
I told her too, how constant prayer
Might glad us in the woodlands there,
Till young devotion on bright wing
  Might bear our raptured souls above,
Or angel forms might gladly bring
  Down to our hearts their peace and love.

V.

" Hush ! thou art weary !" said the maid,—
  " But must not talk of wealth or fear ;
" The monarch's crown, or tyrant's blade,
  " Must never awe thy spirit here !
" 'Tis good to pray to God above,
" 'Tis good to dwell in peace and love,
" But life's stern duties now demand
" A fervent heart and constant hand ;
" For God's own image is defaced,
" And grovelling man hath sunk debased ;
" And lust for power and thirst for gold
  " Hath marked the earth with direful ban,
" Where erst high souls of heavenly mould
  " Had freed and raised their fellow man.

" Hast thou not told me many a tale
" Of dauntless minds who ne'er could fail ;
" But sternly with unflinching eye
" Denounced the deeds of tyranny ;
" And on their quenchless hopes relying
" Ne'er shrunk with craven dread of dying ;
" Whom state nor honour e'er could tempt,
" Who trod on gold with proud contempt,
" Taught men to feel as men, and broke
   " The charms by which the despot sought
" To bind their hands in slavish yoke,
   " To rule the soul and chain the thought.
" And I have dreamed for many an hour
" That thou too Franco hast the power ;
" And if at times thy frame may sink,
" In spirit thou must never shrink ;
" For Franco, I could never love
   " A being sprung from noblest birth,
" Who, formed with mind to rise above,
   " Could grovel in the lowest earth ;
" Who, when the world demanded all
   " His ceaseless toil and fearless heart,
" Himself could his own powers enthrall
   " In selfish ease and live apart."

VI.

Oh ! sweetest music was the voice
   Of Hilda on that glorious morn ;
It seemed to bid each sense rejoice,
   Though sick and weary, faint and worn.
'Twas sacred as the minstrel's spell
   When played before the Hebrew King,
And, as the holy legends tell,
   Banished his dark imagining.

But of those joys I saw my last,
I know not how they came or passed ;
For tho' I may tread o'er again
My bygone years of guilt and pain,
And feel the pang of many an hour
  In all that long and dreary track ;
Yet fancy now hath lost the power
  To call the bliss of moments back.

VII.

'Twas at the calm of evening time
  I left my Hilda's fragrant bowers ;
Whilst shadows from some holier clime
  Fell on my heart like dew on flowers.
The sun had sunk behind the hill,
And vale and woodland all were still ;
Whilst saddened thought and fond regret
For her whom I so late had met,
Mingled with hopes of purest birth,
Wafted me from this lower earth.
But soon alas ! these heavenly dreams
Felt the gross flame of worldly beams ;
And gold, red gold, before me flushed,
And glittering scenes before me rushed.
Visions of all that wealth could buy
Flashed brightly on my dazzled eye.—
The monarch's crown and noble's name,
Titles and honour, glory, fame,
With all that sense or soul could want,
Or pampered tyranny could vaunt.—
Thrones, powers, dominions, gorgeous state !
  The riches of the seas and mines !
Castles and temples rich and great,
  Tall places like golden shrines,

Perfumes and cedars and rare gems,
Rings, sceptres, chains and diadems ;—
Bright Tyrian robes of silken hue
   Gleaming like heaven with pearls and stars ;—
Fair crystal walls to meet the view,
   With milk-white steeds and ivory cars ;—
High banquettings to please the taste,—
   All meats and wines, all fruits and flowers,
To which e'en mitred heads might haste,
   And where young gods might kill the hours.
Then syren forms and beauty's smiles
Bewitched me with a thousand wiles,
Beckoned me on with jewelled hands
To enter their enchanted lands.
Thus far I dreamed, when lo ! the moon
   Rose coldly, chastely, purely bright ;
And scenes and dreams like stars at noon
   Were lost amid the queenly light.
And then fair Hilda's form divine,
   Like morn upon the troubled wave,
Subdued each vain desire of mine,
   And gentler scenes to fancy gave.

VIII.

Days passed away, whilst doubts and fears,
And changing hopes and schemes and tears,
By turns flew headlong through my brain,
Then softened in my heart like rain.
Weeks passed : that lonely tower was mine ;
   Ay, wholly mine, for none would dare
To set their foot within that shrine,
   Or pass the path that led men there.
For tales were told that Satan's rout
Danced ever that drear place about ;

And demon troops of various hue
   Oft seized poor pilgrims for their prey ;
But what 'twas for, or what to do,
   The truthful tellers ne'er could say.
Such wild romance I ne'er denied,
   But knelt at mass and bent to cross ;
Enriched the convents far and wide,
   Counted my gain and reeked not loss.

IX.

Back to my college home I went,
With fevered will and strange intent ;
For ghastly shapes and glittering schemes
Inflamed me aye with constant dreams.
Vainly the house of prayer I trod,
Gold was my idol, gold my god ;
And books and lore were lost to me
In one dread tome of sorcery.
All shapes and forms that met my view
Were tinged by one unhallowed hue.
The clouds that hung in sunset fair
Seemed golden castles in the air ;
Rivers and lakes were molten gold
Refined within a burning mould ;
And if in visions of the night
Fair Hilda's form e'er blest my sight,
Bright gold beamed o'er her every dress
To hide or shade her loveliness.
Red gold was grafted in my soul
Till conscience lost its wise control ;
Or, if at times it woke from rest,
'Twas but to sting and fire my breast.
My hours in golden dreams were frittered ;
In every thought they gleamed and glittered ;

And whilst I revelled in the sight
Of golden piles and treasure bright,
I chafed to find my hand restrained,
And burned to spend the gold I'd gained.

X.

Where were my aspirations then ?
   Those high desires of holy birth,
Those hopes to teach my fellow men,
   And raise them from their native earth ?—
Where was that peace aforetime given,
That joy in Hilda, God, and heaven ?—
All vanished in a desert wind
Which left but arid waste behind !

XI.

But this was madness, frenzy, fever,—
Such torture could not last for ever :
Each evil wish grew strong and bold ;
I could have plunged in molten gold
To burst the chain and break the check
   That bound my every act and deed ;
I dared to live, and scorned the beck—
   The frown of God, or curse of creed.
But first I sinned in small degree ;
   And sorely did the tempter tempt,
Ere yet in vice I could be free,
   And treat all goodness with contempt.
'Twas wine's seductions first that stole
In poisoned sweetness to my soul.
Then witching glance and beauty bought
Fired my hot blood, and drove my thought
From Hilda's love so pure, divine,
So faithfully and wholly mine !

God ! how my heart with anguish burned
When first from virtue's path I turned ;
When I was caught within the wiles
Of syren eyes and wanton smiles.
And then I felt a fool and slave
To passions, which the wise and brave
With chastened mind could aye subdue,
Though Hilda's love they never knew.
But then I drank more wine, and sought
    Such wild companions as could drown
Remorse and conscience, soul and thought,
    Nor reck for judgment, curse or frown.—
Then wildly gamed and threw the dice,
And learnt me every cankering vice,
And lower sunk in deep excess,
And joy that turned to wretchedness.
For purchased smile and poisoned bowl
Could not for ever still my soul ;
But there were times when reason came
And sobered e'en my frenzied frame ;
For fear of hell and awe of death
Can make the valiant suck their breath ;
And terror at the gloomy grave
Can make a coward of the brave ;
But if it seize a trembling slave
To passion's fierce and mad control,
    It haunts him like a deadly blight ;—
A ceaseless gnawing at his soul,
    A fire by day, a fiend by night.

XII.

But there were men, and these I found,
Who trod upon unhallowed ground ;
Who boldly God and heaven defied,
And swore His sacred word had lied ;

And many a sage, whose tomes I saw
    Upon my uncle's secret shelves,
Who set aside each creed and law
    And taught another plan themselves.
Bruno and Sanchez there I read ;
Agrippa who could raise the dead;
With all Spinoza's mystic lore ;
    Cardan and Georgius, dread and wild ;
And many an ancient author more,—
    Meet teachers for a froward child.
O'er all their ponderous schemes I pored,
With their vain dreams my mind I stored,
And all their subtle reasonings brought
Within the circle of my thought,
Till I could flout each holy creed
    And scoff and sneer at priestly rules ;
And vulture-like on garbage feed,
    And treat good men as slaves and fools.

XIII.

But soon I felt the fearful power
I held in that triumphant hour ;
And burned to work each glittering scheme,
And bring to life each golden dream ;
Collect each earthly joy and pleasure
That could be bought with earthly treasure.
But terror still my hand restrained,
For my great wealth was unexplained ;
And bigot rage and monkish rule
Might seize me as an easy tool ;
Prey on the tempting riches vast
That magic sorcery had amassed,
Unveil my art, denounce each spell,
And curse me with the book and bell ;

Or, raze my palace to the ground
  If I should dare to thwart their aims ;
Or, chained and fettered, tortured, bound,—
  Commit my body to the flames.
Nor was this all, for I would dwell
  On Hilda's love so pure, divine,—
And ever con some plot or spell
  To make her radiant beauty mine.
Tho' in my guilty soul I knew
That she would scorn my show to view ;
And ne'er would yield her heart to me
Amid such vice and luxury ;
Yet in that guilty soul I'd sworn
  That she should be my earthly bride ;
Yes ! though she aye should hate and scorn
  The means that brought her to my side.
All changed was now that pure devotion,
That chastened hope and soft emotion,
Which had erewhile my spirit filled
When Hilda's form my bosom thrilled.
Then 'twas that light which God hath given
To lend to man some taste of heaven ;
A spark of that pure flame which shines
  Around the angel choirs above,
Which softens, purifies, refines
  The very hearts who kneel and love.
But now that flame had vanished hence,
And visions of the grosser sense
Around me like to witchcraft twined,
Whilst passion seized my fallen mind.
I was enslaved—in bondage held,—
I felt my better feelings quelled ;
For whilst of her such dreams I dreamed
  And plotted out such damned designs,
E'en to my tainted self it seemed
  Like sacrilege to sacred shrines ;

And whilst of old to saints I'd prayed
For blessings on that holy maid,
Yet now in this unholy time
I called on fiends to aid my crime.

XIV.

Deep far within the magic ground
That circled my lone tower around,
I found a cavern, dim and vast,
A sepulchre of nations past ;
Where fugitives from savage Huns,
   And bygone beasts of unknown form,
Had left their rusting skeletons
   To crumble in the blast and storm.
The vaulted roofs and gleaming walls
Stretched on in endless range of halls,
Whilst sparkling peaks and radiant spars
Shone like a world of fiery stars.
It was an olden temple where
   Long crowds of worshippers had trod,
To pay within its chambers rare
   Devotion to some idol god ;
And there each ancient throne and shrine
Still glittered in that wondrous mine ;
Sculptured from out the solid rock,
Untouched by time, unmoved by shock ;
Though priests and gods had passed away,
   And kneeling host and victim band
Were turned to dust, the sport and play
   Of nature's ever changing band.
There in that palace of the dead,
Far, far away from mortal tread,
I sought to build my Paradise
For frenzied guilt and frantic vice.

XV.

All joys, all pleasures, all delights
    Sense could desire, or tongue could speak ;
Or fancy in her wildest flights
    Thro' ocean, earth, or air could seek ;
I gathered in that mighty cave
To be—a captive and a slave.
There in those chambers, rich and vast,
An empire's treasures I amassed ; —
There sculptor's art and painter's skill
Were tasked to please my lordly will,
Till triumphs over age and time
Were pictured on my walls sublime ;—
There loveliest form and sweetest tone
Feasted my eyes and ears alone,
With rare perfumes of richest scent,
And beauty's daintiest blandishment.
Gold purchased all !—heart, mind, and soul
Were sacrificed at my control.
The gorgeous East poured forth for me
    Her endless stores and countless slaves ;
And all the wealth of land and sea,
    Through desert wilds and pathless waves,
Were borne to me as offerings meet,
And laid in triumph at my feet.

XVI.

Oh ! 'twas a palace fit to be
A heaven for young divinity :
A world to which the mightiest king
    Who reigns in Indy's orient land,
His crown and power alike might bring
    To live a slave at my command.

No genii home beneath the sea,
  No secret dwelling in the spheres,
No gardens in fair Araby
  Though ceaseless summer glads the years ;—
No ocean caves, nor coral isles,
Where merman loves and mermaid smiles ;—
No golden bowers within the sun,
Though there bright seraphs one by one
Fly off on beams with joyous glee
To wake the stars to harmony ;—
No flowery island in the moon,
  Though beauties from the land of dreams
Danced ever to the liquid tune
  Of zephyr airs and silver streams ;—
Nought ever flashed to mortal eye,
Filled hearts with higher ecstacy,
Or e'er to sense and reason stole
With such soft witcheries for the soul.
Within the vast and glittering halls
Were held perpetual festivals ;
And feast and song and wine and flowers
Gave wings to all the fleeting hours ;
Whilst rarest clouds of rich perfumes
Shed Eastern incense through the rooms.
On couches of bright Tyrian hue,
The wearied form might rest and view
Shapes, fairer than the fairest one
That danced before Belshazzar's throne ;—
A glittering throng of varied charms,
Of melting smiles and tempting arms ;
Whilst countless urns of curious light
  Flung their sweet radiance over all ;
Yet never there, by day or night,
  Was seen the writing on the wall ;

For talismans on every gate,
    And amulets on every neck,
Could tell each dark design of fate
    And every stranger footstep check.

XVII.

Such Paradise I brought to birth
Within the mystic womb of earth ;
And who that saw the outward gloom
Could guess the world within that tomb ?
For all the feasts and banquets bright
Were hurried there at dead of night
By villains, dutiful and bold,
Whom I had bribed with constant gold,
And awed by fearful oath and threat
Which trembling crime can ne'er forget.
And none of all the endless crowd,
That aye before my presence bowed,
E'er knew the door or saw the stair
Which led their willing footsteps there ;
For all in midnight's darkest hour
    Through secret ways were brought or driven,
Yet never sought or sighed for power
    To bear them from that wondrous heaven.

XVIII.

But sick and weary, restless ever,
Tortured and racked by ceaseless fever,
Sated, but never satisfied,
Tho' every day new joys I tried :—
A weight upon my spirit hung,
A knell within my conscience rung,

My eyes with hideous shapes were filled,
My heart with Hilda's love was thrilled.
In vain to every joy I turned
To quench the raging fire which burned ;
I would have bartered all my wealth
For quiet rest and cooling health,
Or e'en to plunge in Lethe's stream
And find three bygone years a dream.
But in that dark and dreary hour
I felt that Hilda still had power.
My worship now was frantic passion ;
   I aimed to bear her to my cave,
Reckless alike of form or fashion ;
     For though in vice I'd grown a slave
     'Gainst virtue I was fierce and brave.
Scarce but three fleeting years had passed
Since in my arms I clasped her last ;
And she had heard that I had gone
To wander through the world alone ;—
Had left my books to study men
Till love should call me home again.
I laid my plan and formed my scheme,
For 'twas to me a constant theme ;
And left my cavern in the night
   Like a foul vampire from his tomb,
To wander in unhallowed flight
   And prey on beauty's holiest bloom.
Oh ! why did not the angel then
Blot out my name from living men ?
Why did not then my life-blood flee,
   Or burst its veins, or change its hue,
Aghast at such vile treachery
   To one so lovely and so true ?
Demons must then with joy have seen
A dastard soul so fallen and mean ;

And weeping angels prayed to heaven
  My false and hardened heart to doom,
Unshrived, unwept, and unforgiven,
  Down to the darkness of the tomb ;
There in the womb of earth to lie
Till God and judgment fill the sky.

———

Canto III.

I.

It was that calm and quiet hour
   When night's first sweets to day are given ;
When vale and mountain, wood and flower,
   Feel the first breath of summer even ;
That filled with black designs I rode
To seek my Hilda's fair abode.
Her father was a soldier brave,
Who early met a soldier's grave ;
Her mother was of noble birth,
With fortune smaller than her worth ;
Who lived apart, and reared her child
   In all the virtues of her race ;
Whilst heaven upon the maiden smiled
   In loveliest youth and holiest grace.
To their fair Eden home I went
With reptile heart and mean intent ;
And when to that pure shrine I came,
   Men might have seen, if men might view
A serpent heart transform the frame,—
   A demon of the darkest hue.

II.

Alone I passed the sacred place,
Where last I gazed on Hilda's face :
Alone I passed our trysting bower,
But all was silent at that hour ;
No sound came murmuring through the trees
Save distant rill and evening breeze.

I sought the house ;—an old nurse told
How Hilda's mother, worn and old,
That morn was carried to the tomb,
A victim to her destined doom.
No more the crone would say or tell,
But instantly I bribed her well.
She whispered, as she felt the gold,
   That grief had wasted Hilda's cheek ;
And on the morn with purpose bold
   The maiden would the convent seek.

III.

No flattering speech or fervent prayer
Could gain me then admittance there.
I heard the voice of priestly men,
And what cared I for priestcraft then ?
But death to me were certain fate
Should priest but find my cavern gate ;
So fear restrained the hand and deed
Which ne'er were bound by God or creed.
To Hilda's ear my name was borne,
   But Hilda would not see or hear,
Yet faintly promised that at morn
   She'd meet me in the garden near,
Ere yet within the convent's cell
She tombed the heart I loved so well.

IV.

Stunned, stupified, and motionless,
O'ercome by dark and strange distress,
Oppressed and chilled by sudden gloom
As though I then had heard my doom,

Again I passed the garden gate,—
All reckless, cheerless, desolate,
As though a seraph hand had driven
My spirit from this Eden heaven.
The night was passed, I know not how,
And morn was bright on leaf and bough ;
When once again those bowers I entered,
Where all my life and soul were centred.

V.

I see her now with pallid cheek,
    Drooping and pale with recent tears ;
Trembling as when she same to seek
    Him the young hope of bygone years.
Oh bear the ghostly vision hence !
    For ever on my path it glares,
Preying upon my reason—sense ;—
    I must away !— I have no prayers !—
But I will face it ! aye I must,
Tho' on this spot I turn to dust !
Thou art a dream !—I will be brave !—
And thou art mouldering in thy grave !
Fiends, angels help me !—'tis for this
I' ve dared recall each scene of bliss ;
And if I can but turn and face
    Thee,—spirit of the torturing past !—
Content me that my heart is base,
    And reck not fortune's smile or blast,
I yet may find one guilty man
More cursed than I was or am,
Nor feel that I am doomed to be
The worst in hell's dark company.

VI.

Oh, look not with those pleading eyes !
　Nor let forgiveness pale thy brow !
　Oh could I weep one tear drop now,
I straight should be in Paradise.
Ye angels in your holy spheres !
Oh let me shed one burst of tears !
Out from my soul the demon drive,
And let one dying spirit live !
Let me be smote with every pain
Save madness in my whirling brain !
Let all earth's worst and fiercest woes,
Hunger and thirst, or fever's throes,
Save conscience with her constant din,
Be just reward for all my sin !
But then, oh let me be forgiven !
But stay !—Can I meet her in heaven ?—
Oh God from off Thy awful throne
List to a sinner's bursting groan !
Ere from this earth you give release
Soften this heart and give me peace.

VII.

One pang, one moment scarce it seems,
　Since Hilda last my presence sought ;
For guilt hath mingled facts and dreams
　All madly in my wildering thought ;
Yet every word and sigh she uttered,
And e'en the false replies I muttered,
I know, and aye must know, and feel
Deep in my breast like poisoned steel.

" Franco !" she said, " why dost thou seek
     " A stranger maiden at this hour ?
" But stay ! of love thou must not speak,
     " Nor breathe of passion in this bower !
" The time is passed ; for I am given
" To be the humble bride of heaven !
" You chose your path ;—it leads to death !
     " You sacrificed to low desires
" The soul God gave you with his breath,
     " Which erewhile glowed with holy fires !
" Then wherefore dost thou seek me now ?
     " The memory of this spot will be
" But doubling of thy pain when thou
     " Shalt waken to thy misery.
" Then haste !—say what thou wilt and go ;
" Nor grieve me more, nor swell thy woe !"

VIII.

Though trembling like a coward slave,
I tried to speak with purpose brave :—
" Hath foul mouthed slanderers dared to grieve
     " Thy spirit with their falsest lie ?
" And Hilda, can thy heart believe
     " In such excess of calumny ?
" Some cunning monk with demon sneer
" Hath tampered with thy willing ear !
" Time was I would have scorned and laughed
" At such display of priestly craft ;
" And thou too Hilda would have been
" Incensed at treacheries so mean ;
" And would have spurned the lips that sought
" With such deceit to fill thy thought !
" And dost thou doubt my faith and truth ?
" I, who have loved from earliest youth,—

" Since first our infant hands were laid,—

" Cease, cease this mockery!" cried the maid ;—
" Hast thou not sold to frantic vice
" A soul once fit for Paradise—
" That mind and power that erst were given
" To aid the high designs of heaven ?
" And there are tales in fearful wise
" Which speak of darker mysteries —

" A monkish lie !' I feebly cried :—
" Oh hear me first, and then decide :
" Through many a distant clime I've been,
" And many a wild and wondrous scene ;
" For all the stores of gold were mine
" Which lay within my uncle's shrine.
" And now that I have ceased to roam,
" I've built me up a secret home,
" To hoard the wonders, which my hand
" Had gathered round from every land ;
" And idle head, or vulgar fear,
" Hath coin'd the tale which met thy ear.
" Oh Hilda ! I have loved thee ever,
" Thy form hath left my spirit never ;
" And thou hast been my life and light,
" Till pure desires of heavenly flight,
" And lofty hopes and noble schemes
" Were twined with thee in all my dreams ;
" And never was my heart estranged,
" And never hath my love been changed !
" Then, wilt thou spurn me for a lie,
" A nurse's rhyme or calumny ?
" And Hilda, I have endless power ;
" Thrones, crowns, and empires are thy dower :

" For in my uncle's lonely cell
" Were treasures which no tongue can tell ;
" Wealth which can vanquish land and sea,
   " And buy all titles, fame, and worth ;
" Till every nation bend the knee
   " And make us gods upon the earth ;
" Tyrants shall shrink before thine eye
" And dastard guilt from thee shall fly,
" Till empires feel thy fostering hand
" And goodness dwells in every land.
" Then will we burst the bonds and chains
" Where gloomy superstition reigns ;
" Root out each bigot faith and creed
   " And light the world with reason's ray ;
" Till man, from every shackle freed,
   " Shall hail the beam and bless our sway.
" Oh Hilda ! hear my prayer and vow !
" If e'er I've ceased to love thee now,
" Or fail to love thee from this hour,
" May death and fortune blast my power,
" And every ill that mortals see
" Heap on me all their misery.
" Then Hilda, take my heart and soul !
" Bend all my thought to thy control !
" The world with all its store is thine,
" If thou wilt be but wholly mine ;
" Each wish, each hope shall be fulfilled,
   " And all the dreams of early youth
" That e'er within our bosoms thrilled,
   " Shall spring to life and live in truth."

IX.

An eye of scorn looked on me now,
A haughty lip and queenly brow ;

For whilst so fair and free from guile,
She saw each false and lying wile,
And knew, whilst her young heart was swelling,
Each cunning lie my lips were telling.
But yet one deathless feeling strove,
One glimmering spark of sacred love,
One bitter tear, one fond regret
For one she never could forget ;
For that pure flame which beams on high
When kindled here can never die,
Nor time, nor wrong extinguish it,
When once within the soul 'tis lit ;
By it all life's best charms are given,
    And if beset by cold despair,
It bears the broken heart to heaven,
    To glow for aye in rapture there.
She knew that all her dreams had fled,
She felt that all her hopes were dead,
But yet one glance of pity fell
With holy charm and heavenly spell ;
As though an angel ever slept
In her soft eyes, but woke and wept
When'er a thing of evil hue
Dared to' approach her chastened view.
But love like evil may be masked
If all the powers of soul be tasked ;
And none the torturing thought may know,
Nor see the depth of hidden woe,
But they who mark the stricken heart,
And note the sigh, the tear, the start ;
And doubly damned that soul shall be,
    And mine be blasted with the rest,
That e'er would plant such misery
    Within so young and pure a breast.

X.

Though from her eye the tear came down,
Yet sorrow could not check the frown :—
" Oh Franco ! is it come to this ?
" And dost thou dare to talk of bliss ?
" And must thou act a masquer's part
" To hide the evil of thy heart ?
" And stoop to arts so mean and wild,
" As would be mockery to a child ?
" Thy lip, thy cheek, thy brow, thy eyes
" Bespeak the excess thy tongue denies ;—
" Thy store of gold is nought to me,
" But what thou sayest is sorcery ;
" For magic power alone could bring
    " Such treasures as thou callest thine,
" And not for wealth which decks a king
    " Would e'er I name such riches mine.
" And see ! thy soul hath fallen so low,
" That e'en thyself doth scarcely know
" The dark debasement of thy mind,
" The fetters which thy spirit bind.
" The shame which prompts thy speech, betrays
" The evil of thy thoughts and ways.
" Gold is thy god, and to its beams
" Thou'st sacrificed thy hopes and dreams,
" Yielded thy life with trembling fear,—
" Yea ! brought thy glittering idol here,
" And worshipped it before my face,
" To dazzle me with golden grace ;
" But none but beings fallen as thou
" At such a gew-gaw shrine could bow !
" Hath ever yet thy boasted wealth
" Calmed thy lost soul, or brought thee health ?

" Thy haggard cheek and feverish eye
" Would such presumptuous hopes belie !
" And say, what glory ever came
" From grovelling, gold-begotten fame ?—
" A beam where cringing slaves may flock
" With lips to praise but hearts to mock !
" Go ! learn of all the bygone great
" Of boundless power and endless state,—
" The tyrant king, or warrior god,
" Who left, where'er their feet have trod,
" The best blood of the good and brave,
" Or fetters for the vanquished slave,—
" Who vainly deemed their names sublime
" Must live through death and conquer time !—
" Where are they ?—vanished with their age !
" Scarce left on history's dustiest page !
" But they,—-the high, the glorious throng,
" Who live in science, arts, and song,—
" Outlive the crash of empires past,
" The earthquake's storm and tempest's blast !
" No gilded temple guards their fame,
" No lofty column bears their name,
" Their dust can scarce their times survive,
" But with the world their deeds shall live.
" No Cæsar and no Crœsus they,
    " No conquering chief of Macedon ;
" They sought not tyrant power and sway,
    " Nor blood and gold of empires won :
" But they have freed the mind, and taught
" The liberty of quenchless thought,
" The government of erring sense,
" And virtue's true omnipotence ;
" That man might know himself, and feel
    " His destiny and high descent ;
" Might leave the gold and sheath the steel,
    " And labour on with brave intent

" To gain that chief, that crowning goal—
" Perfection for the human soul !
" And long as hearts can feel and glow,
" Long as the mind can learn and know,
" Long as the' aspiring thought can love
" Goodness below or God above,—
" Their memories like the stars shall be
" Emblems of immortality,
" Throwing from realms of darkest night
" A deathless beam and heavenly light.
" Such Franco I had dreamed for thee !
" I said not thou wert false to me ;
" But to thy conscience thou hast lied,
" And all thy promise falsified ;
" Thy soul, thy thought, thy hopes are changed ;
" Thy heart and mind are all estranged ;
" And thou the lowest depths hast trod,
" And dared deny a creed and God,
" With all the cant of atheist fools,
" Fresh from the folly of their schools,
" Who laugh at heaven-born faiths, and pray
" To wisdom and to reason's ray :
" But know ! the idlest creed that's taught
" Is better than their subtlest thought !
" Freedom like their's is rank and vile !
" Fit only for some despot's isle,
" Where naked steel preserves the law
" When God and virtue cease to awe !"

" Such liberty as I have dreamed,
" I cannot tell thee ! it hath beamed
" In visions bright but undefined,
" Like rainbow glory on my mind :
" They've passed ! and Franco we must part !
" Mourn not that thou hast lost my heart !

" But seek to save thy fallen soul
" From sin and Satan's dark control!
" Farewell ! and oh repent and pray
" For all the errors of thy way !
" Rely on God's all pardoning love,
" And think—we yet may meet above :"

XI.

How felt I then ?—I cannot tell !
    For mingled madness, pain, and ire,
Had turned my conscience to a hell ;—
    Till burning thoughts like things of fire
Reeled in the tempest of my brain ;
    And my hot, hissing blood was sent
Boiling yet scorching thro' each vein
    Like lightning thro' a firmament.
My heart was now before me laid,
Not in its own disguise arrayed,
But stript of every flimsy dress
And naked in its rottenness.
Nor was this all : I could have borne
    To see that thing before me cast ;
Recked not that I was foul and lorn,
    Though then I must have shrunk aghast ;
But I was lowered in the sight
Of one I loved—my life, my light !
And then the thought that she had seen
Each plague spot there, each foul gangrene ;
    And knew full well, to say the best,
The fool and madman I had been :
    God ! it all rankled in my breast !
I covered and trembled in the gaze
    Of Hilda's scorn and Hilda's eye,
Like a vile traitor in the blaze
    Of late discovered treachery.

XII.

Pale, pure and holy—there she stood,
   Like a good angel, from some sphere
Sent down with heavenly power endued
   To teach or strike vain mortals here;
All sacred as some mystic shrine
Guarded by saintly forms divine.
My coward schemes all failed me then;
I shrunk abashed beneath her ken,
And looked upon her as a God,
Whilst slowly o'er the dewy sod
With one last look she turned away,
With quivering lip that seemed to pray.
I marked her drooping spirit there,
Whilst heaven seemed struggling with despair;
But as she passed an ivied seat,
In olden time our loved retreat,
She fell as with the weight of years;
   I sprung like lightning to her side:
A flood of wild resistless tears
   Burst from her eyes in stormy tide:
She shivered like an aspen leaf,
Then fainted with excess of grief.
I caught her in my frantic arms!
   Light as a feathered bird she pressed:
But when I felt her youthful charms
   All glowing to my burning breast,
Once more my fiendish plots and schemes
Fired through me with electric beams.
I bore her through the garden gate;
   No sense nor feeling had she now;
Knew not her life, nor saw her fate,
   Yet trembled like a woodland bough
When shook by midnight wind and thunder,
Its life and strength half snapt asunder.

My saddled horse I quickly found ;
  Still in my arms my Hilda lay ;
Onward we sprung with fleetest bound,—
  I lost my soul but won my prey.

XIII.

I was a madman at that hour,
With whirling brain and demon power !
I heard a noise of men behind,
But dashed on swifter than the wind.
The form that lay upon my breast
Woke for one instant from her rest,
And gazed around, but tree and stream
Flashed by us like a drunken dream ;
And all unknowing as the dead
She sunk again, whilst on we sped ;
Till halting near a blackened thicket
I oped my cavern's secret wicket,
Led in my steed, and bore my prey,
And set all outward foes at bay.

XIV.

By wild excitement racked and torn,
  By dark mysterious fears oppressed ;
Flushed, feverish, weary, faint, and worn,
  And sick and cold from want of rest,
I scarce could move without a groan ;
  To woman hand the maid I gave :
And crawling to a cushioned throne,
  I ordered every cringing slave

Upon a couch her form to lay,
And watch and tend her night and day ;
And at the moment when her sense
Recovered its intelligence,
One of the fleetest knaves should bring
The tidings to their cavern king.

XV.

Wine in a maddening, burning stream,
     I drank with parched and cracking throat ;
When lo ! strange glances seemed to gleam,
     And stranger forms before me float.
Was I betrayed ?—the fearful thought
With deadly horror was enwrought.
I gazed around—a shivering thrill
Filled me with dread of nameless ill.
I knew each visage there, yet saw
That hate was mingled with their awe,
And fancied I could clearly trace
Some black design on every face.
I sent for those whose eyes and smiles
Had caught me deepest in their wiles ;
But now each yielding lovely slave
Was dark and solemn as the grave.
I called my guards, and bribed the hands
Of all my bravest, trustiest bands ;
But every man of all the clan
Seemed marked by some unearthly ban,
And nothing said and nought would tell,—
Their lips were closed by glamour spell.
Once more from out my vest I took
My uncle's clasped and secret book,
To see if its contents had power
To tell the dangers of that hour !

I pored, till lo ! a verse I read,
Dire as the language of the dead,
Which reached my eye and filled my sense
With terrible intelligence ;
For thus it ran and thus it told
What horrors I must soon behold :—

" Three years only may bain man
" Rule the forms of spirit scan !
" Three years only may he wield
" Spirit powers to guard and shield !
" Where shall then the mortal go ?
" Not till then shall mortal know !"

Swifter than thought I numbered years,
Then days as countless as my fears ;
When on my soul the sentence burst
   That this dark day must be my last ;
For since I read that volume first
   Three fleeting, fevering years had passed ;
And on that very midnight hour
I must yield up my spirit power.

XVI.

Not yet had Hilda reached her life,
To feel earth's pain or know its strife !
Not yet could leech or nurse impart
Such blessing to her fainting heart !
Eight hours to midnight !—must I leave her ?
   The maddening fact—the stinging thought—
Lashed up my brain to frantic fever,
   Till hope and love alike were nought.

XVII.

" Bring wine," I cried, " to drown all fear
    " And rouse the dull intelligence !
" Let music fill the languid ear,
    " And beauty fire the torpid sense !
" Let forms, like pleasure's handmaids wait,
    " And bring new draughts of heavenly bliss
" Who heeds the hour, or recks their fate,
    " Upon a night so bright as this ?
" Awake ! awake ! the song and bowl
" Shall charm the mind and feast the soul !
" Up to the mirthful dance arise
" With glowing cheeks and sparkling eyes ;
" And foot it lightly to the strain,
" Till smiles and laughter banish pain !
" The lamps burn dim !—more fair and high
    " Pour out the streams of incensed fire !
" Our cave shall match a summer sky,
    " Or we within its flames expire !
" Now rend the air with louder tones
    " And shame the angel choirs above !
" Let beauty share our cups and thrones
    " And earth be lost in looks of love ;
" And let me take this shading tress
" Of rich surpassing loveliness,
" And sweep the care from off my brow
" Till I can breathe a passioned vow !
" Let orient fragrance fill the rooms,
" And rarest scents and soft perfumes
" Float in dim clouds through every hall ;
    " And let our evening feast be spread !
" We'll hold a gorgeous festival
    " Would tempt a god or wake the dead !"

Such were my ravings at that hour ;
And there I ruled a sovereign still,
O'er slaves who felt my wealth and power,
And bent submissive to my will.

XVIII.

The dance was o'er ! the feast was laid !—
All meats and cates, all fruits and flowers,
From fertile mead and garden glade,
From Indian groves and Persian bowers.
The smiles were spells ! the songs were charms
To win the soul to pleasure's arms !
And brighter, gayer grew the smiles
And softer music woke the aisles.
When lo ! a wild and fearful shout
Was heard our cavern gates without,
Piercing alike our doors and walls,
And thundering thro' our vaulted halls ;
Whilst force, like that of earthquake shook,
Seemed struggling in the earth beneath,
Ready to burst the solid rock
Which held us in its mighty teeth.
Then shrieks and cries where echoed loud
From all my cavern's gathered crowd ;—
The feast and dance alike were left,
And all, of sense and reason reft,
Rushed, screamed, and fainted through the halls
Till madness filled the trembling walls.
Slaves sprung to me with steel and brands
All naked in their frantic hands ;
Flung off allegiance,—loudly swore
Relief that instant must be given,
Or my heart's blood should stain the floor
To stay the vengeful wrath of heaven.

XIX.

The fumes of wine were in my brain,
   And conscience now was forced to rest ;
I felt not then a sting or pain,
   For courage filled and nerved my breast.
To all the mob I spoke at length
Of all my wealth and skill and strength ;
And swore if they would stand and dare
I could defy an army there ;
Ay, that the gods might dread my power
E'en at that wild and gloomy hour.
Thus awed I left the stricken crowd,
   And hurried to the secret gate ;
But there large bands of horsemen proud
   With noisy clatter seemed to wait,
All vainly seeking for the door
To lead them to my cavern floor.
This I did neither heed nor reek !
   I knew my glamour might sublime
Could every mortal footstep check
   Till midnight's dark and fated time.

XX.

Swift through my head like lightning beams
Flashed a whole train of headlong schemes ;
For I was like a captive bound
   By troops above and spells below ;
With fools and drunken knaves around
   Who dared not strike a single blow.
I must away that very night,
And Hilda too must share my flight ;
Yet if the mob who swelled my state
Once lit upon my cavern gate,

They all with deadly haste would speed,
  As though a fiend were in their rear ;
Nor bribes nor threatenings hear or heed
  With foes so close and death so near.
And then the frantic crush for life
  That soldier band would rouse and wake ;
And I must fall amid the strife,
  Or perish at the torturing stake.

XXI.

Within my ears I heard the roar,
Yet hurried thro' a corridor
To seek the room where Hilda lay,
And bear her fainting form away ;
When lo ! I heard a traitor slave
  Parleying with eager troops without ;
With one fierce thrust I slew the knave
  And straight rejoined my coward rout.
For I had thought that none had known
That entrance but myself alone ;
And well I knew one rebel hand
Might ope the gate to all the band.

XXII.

One glance !—I saw my power was o'er,
  My amulets had lost their light !
One pang my heaving bosom tore
  Ere I regained my nerve and might.
One gate that soldier band had found !
  I heard them clattering on the stair ;
One door remained, and with one bound
  I yet might force an exit there.

" Now !" cried I to my trembling slaves :—
" Ye who have feared your deaths and graves
" I go for arms which will defy
" Alike the gods of earth or sky !"
With one wild spring I left the hall
   With whirling brain and maddened reel ;
   And fleet as lightning seeks the steel
I dashed along by door and wall ;
And reached the room where Hilda lay
Alone, beneath one pale lamp's ray.
I caught her in my arms, but lo !
   I clasped a corpse all cold and dead !
With fear I staggered to and fro,
   And raised her form, but life had fled.
My horror was beyond all telling ;
The red blood from her heart was welling ;
Her long hair streamed upon her breast ;
Her arms hung down but not at rest ;
Her cheeks were white, and death's eclipse
   Had veiled the light of her still eyes ;
And pallid brow and livid lips
   Told that her soul had sought the skies.
'Twas all too much for man to bear !
I could not meet that ghastly stare,
Nor tamely view at dead of night
That sunken form and sudden blight ;
Nor see my idol and my prey !
   Who but for me were now my bride,
Thus wildly, fouly torn away
   A murdered victim from my side.
My eyes swam round, my senses fled ;
   A sickly stupor seized my frame ;
I fell upon the floor for dead,
   Struck down by fear and crushed by shame ;
And lost in dreams of nameless woe
All heed for life or care for foe.

XXIII.

A mighty noise was thundered round,
  I started to my trembling feet!
I heard a step—a spring—a bound—
  But stayed not with my foes to treat.
A soldier's hand was on the door ;
  A moment passed and bright steel flashed ;
His form lay stretched upon the floor
  As from that fated room I dashed.
I heard a shriek and gathering cry,
And troops and swords came clattering nigh,
But spurred by fear I onward sped,
  And pressed and panted for my life
Sharp thro' a narrow way, which led
Windingly from that cavern dread,
  And gave more equal chance in strife.
I passed it, but was forced to wait
One moment at the secret gate :
My fingers could not find the spring ;
  Ten thousand fiends were in my rear ;
In vain I sought the covered ring,
  My fierce pursuers drew more near :—
The foremost rushed ! my trusty blade
His carcass on the pavement laid ;
I scarce regained my vantage ground,
  For on they pressed, nor gave me grace ;
When straight the hidden lock I found,
  Sprung through, and slammed it to their face.

XXIV.

That fearful night was cold as death,
  And dreary as a yawning tomb.
With clammy brow and quickened breath
  I plunged amid the thickened gloom.

A fell commotion shook the earth,
As though some things of monstrous birth
Convulsed its womb with mighty storms,
To break the walls which held their forms.
A frightened horse came prancing round,
   Without a rider on its back ;
I caught its reins, and with a bound
   I gained a seat and found a track.
On, onwards, fleeter than the wind
   When coursing o'er a desert plain,
I left all foes and fears behind,
   Nor had a care nor felt a pain.

XXV.

I stood upon the lone sea strand
A fishing boat at my command ;
For in my dress were jewels rare
   And golden wealth, a glittering store ;
And I had bribed a sailor there
   To bear me from that fatal shore.
The blackened billows foamed and rolled,
And all was deathly dark and cold,
And brine was on our bosoms splashed,
As o'er the waves our vessel dashed.
Towards my cave I turned one gaze,
   When lo ! with one wild earthquake shock
Arose a bright and lightning blaze
   With voice of thunder from the rock ;
The solid hills were rent and riven,
The flames flashed fiercely up to heaven,
The light of noon lit up the skies,
My ears drank in unearthly cries,
Strange thoughts came rushing through my brain,
An agonizing, torturing train.

I sank !—but more I cannot tell—
In that lone boat insensible.

XXVI.

A convent's cell is my abode;
  A shirt of hair my garment now ;
My conscience ever bears a load,
  And guilt not years hath ploughed my brow ;
My days are spent in prayers and fasting,
My nights in torments everlasting ;
For madness oft will check devotion
And bid me curse each soft emotion ;
Or unbelief within my breast
  Will fiend-like scoff my prayers and creed,
At God and heaven and judgment jest,
  And sneer at each repentant deed.
Within my heart dark thoughts are stinging,
Within my soul a knell is ringing,
Until I'd yield my very life
To quit this ceaseless storm and strife ;
Wer't not that nameless shivering fears,
And teachings of my early years,
Conjure such horrors in the grave,
  Such demons in the yawning tomb,
As would drive back the wise and brave
  If fain to pierce its awful gloom.

L'Enboy.

Within the chapel's sacred wall
Where pictured saints from windows fall;
Beneath the chancel's marble pave,
   Our pious brother Franco lies,
Who in his youth was wild and brave,
   But in his age was good and wise.
Though none hath known from whence he came
   And none his early life can tell;
Save what he in this page may name,
   Or told at his confessional.
'Twas said that he had dealt in spells,
But yet he gave our convent bells;
And that he scoffed at things divine,
But yet he built our Lady's shrine;
And that in heart he scorned to pray
But yet he knelt both night and day.
And when his dying hour was nigh
   Our Abbot aye was at his side;
And watched alone with constant eye
   Until our pious brother died.
Our Abbot now hath sought his rest;
We found this parchment on his breast;
But never into human ear
   One word of Franco hath he told;
And now that each hath sought his bier
   No other thing can time unfold.

www.ingramcontent.com/pod-product-compliance
Lightning Source LLC
Chambersburg PA
CBHW031247260626
47169CB00007B/2490